I Loved

You Here

I Loved You Here

A Book of Poetry

Julianna Balducci

Contents

Note From The Writer   6

Dedication   7

I. THE MORAL COMPASS

Playground Injuries   10

Change   12

Coming Down Snow   13

Olympus   15

Getting Even   17

Ruined Your Christmas   19

Play God   21

End of the Line   24

Skeletons   27

Stay Clean   29

Turn Back The Clock   32

II. ASHES OR CONFETTI

Fatal Attraction   37

Phone   41

Periphery   44

Treasure Chest Closed   45

The Final Girl   48

As Far As Landslides Go 53

Tourist 56

The Good One 60

Swimming Pool Shark 63

Gold Star 66

Holiday 70

Mountain Peaks 74

III. THE RABBIT HOLE

Really in it Now 79

Outlaw 81

Clean Cut 84

Orchard Road 86

Do You Want To Run Away? 88

The Truth Is 91

Shoot First 94

Taylor 95

The Weather App 97

The Archeologist 99

Cheetah in a Cage 102

Fake Our Deaths 104

Bird on the Wire 107

Better You 111

Start a War 113

Camelot 116

The Middle Man   119

Dog-Eared   122

Never Cold   123

In This Life   125

Default   126

The Music All About You   129

Signs of You   130

Dead Man Walking   134

Please!!!!!!   136

Snow Globe   138

Kind of Love   141

Victorian Ghost   147

London Fog   151

Acknowledgements   154

NOTE FROM THE WRITER

For all the desperate moments we beg our friends to retell us stories we have already heard, in desperate hopes of finding a new angle to dissect. Those nights spent up, feverishly being kept awake by someone's mind, with conversations about what you really think makes the sky blue and why you really think you've let your father down. And those moments you can't translate to anyone else, the ones that belong to two people, whose fate was like a wishbone. For all the endless effervescent times spent believing in something good because someone believed in you. Never being cold because you were with someone who made you feel glowy and warm. Traveling to new countries, taking photographs that will never be seen again. And for the very first moment the spark is ignited, when you momentarily ignore the chaos you know is about to ensue…here's a whole book.

DEDICATION

To the niche corners of the world where I loved you so.

From the sidewalks of my childhood neighborhood, to the couch of my college apartment in Iowa, to the cobblestone streets of Ireland…and so on and so forth…

This is it, I loved you here.

The Moral
Compass

Playground Injuries

Two kids unaware of our future history
Playground injuries
That faded to broken heart scars
I could run but never too far
You've always known all my hiding spots
I'm always broken
But your love came easy
At no cost

Two kids lost at sea
Drowned out the echoes with alcohol and
weed
The best kept secret
This movie I've watched it
And I cut it close
Chose the wrong one
That summer was cold knowing I derailed
us
But I only act on impulse
Bandaid patchwork for all my deep cuts
Looking out the window at a world that
could be ours on the bus
With you, I'm never lost
Big dreams and you know them all
I'd do anything to make yours come true

They always ask what was the moment you knew
For me, it was under cloudy chevron skies
A sapphire canvas
Oh, up the coast we were cold
But in the pocket of my coat you left me a note
Past, present, and future history
Every playground injury
Mended and proved you'd always stay

Change

People really do change
And people really do let go
You swore to me you'd always be front row
So what do I do now that you didn't show?

I wished you happy birthday
But I almost wish that I didn't
Because now another girl is in the place I
used to fit in

Everything's monochrome in a shade of
innocence
That has blistered into every-now-and-thens
And protocol 'how have you beens?'
I used to think it would be forever
But we pitched our tent on a forest fire
Keep telling myself it's for the better
I'm a good liar

Now you're footprints in the sand
And I'm tire tracks
You held my hand
But I had your back

But I'll never forget your name
You're the love I'll always know

Coming Down Snow

A haunted moon
A billboard sign
Skipping pennies
Pretending you're mine
Gone too soon
Wishing wells
Ever notice how everything fell
Apart and then back together
I feed the river my tears
Just a worn-in jacket and a couple more
beers
My shoulders sank
The weight was too much
Fill in the blank: I wrote in *"love"*
And the trees they begged
For me to climb them
Get some perspective
Running low
Nearly running out
Raise a glass
Let somebody down
Break the spell
Let it go
Better off with no grudge
To hold
Hands are full

Coming up roses
Coming down snow

Olympus

If you're really sorry you'd be here tonight
Except I'm nowhere to be found when the
timing is right
But jump for the edge and I'll pull my
weight
But it's no surprise that the person I pull up
has my face
Even if I'm failing I'd still blame you

Stand outside the church and try to believe
in peace
But you're the one who gave it to me
And now you can't be seen

I find the courage to call you when I'm
pouring a second glass
Staring out the window wondering how
things ended up like this

Maybe it's for the better
Maybe things were always supposed to end
this way
But you're like childhood fantasy
Something I believed in emphatically
But now no longer exists
Except in stories I tell to strangers in bars

That night in my car
You got out swearing you'd see me again
There was a chasm of silence that somehow
felt like hope
But it was just the water dripping off my wet
clothes

And now I'm terrified I lost my moral
compass
My true north, guiding me through victories
and missteps
I tripped on the hill trying to climb
Olympus
Claimed I broke all my bones
In hopes you'd take me home

Getting Even

Somewhere along the line, I think in the
winter months
You stopped calling it love
You gave it your all and I gave you silver at
best
If I was feeling generous

But you hated all the weight of mine that
you were carrying
So you just dropped it

I just want to ask you, how did you know
this was the last time?
When did you know this was your last try?
Did I break your fault line first so you had to
break mine ?

How'd you just pack it all up like that?
Will you come back?
Where were you living if you thought I was
stuck in the past?
We both fled California, standing our new
grounds
Everything we lost would never again be
found

Don't act like you're so innocent
You asked questions you already knew the
answers to
And I didn't
The roles reversed
I was the one who had to hurt
You resent me for everything
Was this how you always planned on
leaving?
I messed with your head for years on end
Was leaving me behind your way of getting
even?

Ruined Your Christmas

The words you're speaking sound so good
But you hurt me like I knew you would
Kept you around for Christmastime
You got me a present
But I left it to go look at the lights
Would you still hate me if shit looked
different?
I'm sorry I ruined your Christmas

Catastrophic phone calls on Sunday nights
We both got burned once or twice
But you letting me go brought me back to
life

You said I wasn't your villain
Then am I your enemy?
Did you stop trying to know me because you
thought you already knew me?
Are you full of regret or have you already
placed your bets
For how long will I let it lie?
The season has changed and the flowers
have long since died

Did I outgrow your catastrophic dreams?
And I heard you're back in town

What's the score? I know you're keeping
count
If we're tied, want to drive around and look
at the Christmas lights?

Catastrophic holiday
We both stand in our way
If all's lost, is all forgiven?
Wrap the regret up with a ribbon
I'm sorry I ruined your Christmas

Play God

I woke up from my dreams
Thinking you were right next to me
But you were in a bar halfway across the
country
And I'm so sorry
About your grandma
And I'm so sorry
That I'm selfish enough
To think your grandma's death would get
you to confess your love for me
But if I called you out of the ice-cold
November blue
What would you do?
It's been too long since New Year's Day
But what would you say?

And I'm so sorry
For all the moons I've loved you
101 times in the sky
That's such a long goddamn time
But I guess that's how I'll always feel
The darkness feels so surreal
On days your memory doesn't shout at me I
think the darkness fades a shade or two
But it comes back in tidal waves and
hurricanes

And I'm waiting in a phone booth
Seconds away from dialing your number
unearthed from the catacombs of my veins
I don't believe in fate anymore
Or summer

Three winters ago
On a carousel that never seems to end
The carnival closed down
Been out of business for ages now
But I'm still feeding it my quarters
I'm still riding around on the bad religion I
created
All from the confines of my childhood bed
And all the things left unsaid
Pacific Ocean blue and early November
leaves burning red

My puffer jacket still smells like you
But I haven't seen you in years
Didn't even own it back then
But forgetting doesn't make any sense
Because I can't unlearn what I already
know
I was the first person to meet your dog
Writing endlessly about what I've found and
what I've lost

Washed ashore in every ocean
But you never wash away
You stick like the salt of all the seas
You might have left but you never leave
I have to stop believing I can play god
Thinking I can iron out all the pages torn
and ripped at the seams
And from a mid November slush bring back
a full bloom July green

Every Sunday I've thought of you, without
fail
101 moons leave a trail
All the skies we lived and saw
But I can't play god
My mother told me my heart is in the right
place
But I'm still staring off into space
Trying to rearrange the constellations to how
they were that doomsday
But even if I memorized every sky we lived
and saw
I can't play god

End of the Line

Hey, I kinda feel like calling
I know it's only because I'm falling apart
And I'm feeling guilty
If I showed up at your door, would you see
me?
I don't think you know how much you built
me
You're the lights in my city

I know it's not my place but I'm asking
Mutual friends how you are in passing
I play it off like I'm not grasping
To every word they're saying

Did you think it was me calling,
On the other end of the line?
I just wanted to know if you're doing
alright
When you picked up did your heart skip a
beat, like mine?
I want to ask you what made you change
your mind

I drove by your house 4 times before I
picked you up

Texted you I was outside but I didn't want to
interrupt
You got in with a smile on your face
I tried to ask you what changed
You said nothing happened
I didn't realize that what changed was me
So I kept asking

You called me from the airport
That phone call fell short
I don't blame you for what you said
I cried myself to sleep on top of my bed
I wish I was a better liar
Crossed my heart in the crossfire
I can't blame you for an eye for an eye
Driving up the hill early July
There were no stars in the sky
I know you blame me
You should have said it then
Would have saved us both a little trouble
and time

You looked at me sideways
I've been moving slow
Counting the days
Is this really what we've become?
You and me were a window
One of us always on the outside looking in

One of us always had to know
Fogging up our faces
I don't think I've been seen since

Hey, I kinda feel like calling

Hey, I'm feeling kinda lost

I just want to ask you about your day

And promise breaks

Hey, I bet you're doing great

Out there without me

Just hope you know I'm sorry

Skeletons

You scold me for holding you back
Of course you'd frame it like that
Your great escape was your master plan
I was your sleight of hand

I used to think if I could follow the picture
on the box
Then I'd understand how to complete the
puzzle
I think I could throw the first punch if I had
bigger muscles

But if I'm the villain then you're two fold
Because if my hands are bloody, then yours
are to the bone

If I was your altar then you were my
cathedral
Which makes this a crisis of faith
Crossing out all the words on the page
Because I did everything I was told
But it's bigger than me and it's out of my
control

At nineteen you taught me to be soft
But I didn't chart the stars so I got lost

You always held my hand
And you didn't know the way
But you blazed the trail with me
I took it for granted

At twenty you left me stranded
Just as the wind was cooling off
If I hung your stars then you got tired of
holding me up
And if you were the sun then I acted like the
moon
I caught you in your bluff
But you stopped me as I said I was in love
Because saying it too late is sadly never
enough

The haunting of me is you
Finally saw it through
It was a good run
You're not a ghost but that's how you acted:
Paper thin
Invisible yet everywhere all at once
Your biggest lie was your ultimate bluff
My closet overflowed with skeletons
And now you're one of them

Stay Clean

I know I made mistakes

But there's no point in blame

Because who am I if you don't remember
my name?

Was I in your way?

Were you on your way out?
Did the roles reverse?
Was my mind my blessing?

For me it became a curse

Did I cut off circulation,
Holding on too tight?
Is a part of you still waiting
For the timing to be right?
It's the breaking point

It's been long overdue

Did my idolizations isolate you?
Did I end up being nothing you dreamed but
everything you secretly thought?

When was the last time you called it love
before you called it off?

*When I called your bluff did I
whisper it too soft?*

This is not what I wanted

That can't be my problem anymore

I want to tell you I'm leaving for real

I can't keep coming undone

But I'd do it for you no questions asked
We can't erase the past
Am I not who you wanted?
Who am I supposed to turn to now?

Can't worry about that anymore

Will you come searching for me?

I don't know who I'll find

Who are you expecting?
If I let you down again, will you re-draw the
line?

Why won't you come find me?

I could say the same of you
I'll keep telling you the truth

I want you to know that you're the only
person I want to tell
And I want you to come find me

I've always wanted to find you

Forgive all my negligence
You protect your picket fence

I'm trying to stay clean

From me?

Turn Back the Clock

Muddy your boots
Trace your tracks
Hold my hand
Have my back
Sharing a lie
Keeping a secret
Do you know I'm sorry?
Do you know I still mean it?

Do you remember playing games when the
score didn't matter?
On the Fourth of July climbing up the ladder
We sat on the roof and talked
But deep down you knew that yours wasn't
my favorite chapter

There on the couch
Our fingers covered in frosting
Decorating Christmas cookies your mom
made
The thought of growing up was daunting
Only in fourth grade
Something about it all was so pretty
The way the dining room table sat us all
In old wooden chairs that hurt my back
I wish we could go back

Do you ever miss me?

There in the backyard jumping on your
trampoline
Now your sister is up in Eugene
That makes me feel old
She used to play dolls with me
Do you remember riding our bikes down the
road?
I was embarrassed the first time I wore lip
gloss
You called me out in front of the whole
class
But you said I looked cute as we sat in the
back of the car
You're the first boy who hung my moon and
stars

Now your parents are getting divorced
Used to cook dinners in the kitchen, my
family with yours
I hope you're alright
I'm sorry you heard arguments behind
closed doors
Your mom gets to keep the house you grew
up in
Do you remember us sitting on your bed?

There on the street corner as the sun was setting
There in my bedroom you sat in my favorite chair
Your sister wanted to show you the game we made up
She talked and talked and you just stared at me and I smiled
It was a school night and past our bedtime
See you at school tomorrow
And the day after and so forth
Felt like it was you and me forevermore

Do you remember us in your kitchen right after your eighteenth birthday?
You looked me in the eyes and asked me to stay
Your sister was sleeping in her room
And so we whispered
Haven't seen her since last summer
I really miss her
There in the backseat
Different stages, different phases but it all felt the same
You remembered my middle name there in the restaurant booth
Meeting up in secret when we both got older

You said you missed me too
Do you remember walking me home?
Our fingers brushing as we got closer
Helping you with your future
You watched me read your college
application
Then we played with your dog
And talked about how our graduation was
coming sooner than we thought
Do you remember my jacket pocket?
When you tried to make it better
Do you still have my letter?
Nothing has made sense after November
You hung my galaxies when we were
younger and when we got older
I can't believe all that innocence is over
I'm so grateful that I got to scrape my knees
on the sidewalk covered in our chalk

Anytime you're bored
Come retrace your steps
I'm just around the block
For you I'd always turn back the clock

Ashes or Confetti

Fatal Attraction

I'm subject to fatal attraction
And you'll watch it happen
Because it always happens
Spiraling in old fashion
I didn't mean to have that kind of reaction
But it always happens

If you leave me alone long enough I'll think
you hate me
But I think I've been doing a little better
with that lately
But I'll get attached then run it back
inhumanely

I'm burning alive
And all my smoke signals are double
crossed
My body won't sit still
My mind reaches for any medication
I won't learn patience
Build it up just to let you down
I've been sleeping while the sun is still out

I'll rip out all my stitches to stop the
process

I said I was better, but what if I don't want
this?

Would I be your ten point kill or would you
save that admiration for someone better?
If I fell from grace more gracefully I'd be
more clever
But I don't know better
I knit my stomach into knots trying to make
a blanket
Thinking if I'm warmer maybe I'll make it
Through the end
Of this fatal attraction

You text me while you're out with your
friends
Teaching me to trust again
But now I'm slipping
On my haunting past mistakes

If I pretend to be collected,
Can I leave things how we left it?
I think I'll dig the grave
Then bring flowers to the funeral
Eulogize the mess of it
Seeing double
Blurry vision

Always feel there's something that I'm missing
But if I'm six feet under,
Whose fingerprints are on the shovel?

In two places at once
I thought of running away tonight
But your hand is on my wrist checking my pulse during our little game
Watching the sun come up and falling from new heights

Maybe if I convince myself I'm bored to death I'll leave it be
But I've been thinking too much
There's no cut but I still find a way to bleed
Been anticipating your touch
And you're probably wondering where I run to
And I wish I could tell you that that the smoke is invisible
But finding words is difficult

Maybe if I try to talk it through
I could tell you
Because when you look at me you really see something
Which makes things happen

Moving three steps forward but back one
Spiraling in old fashion
Promise I won't have that kind of reaction
No more fatal attraction

Phone

I'll call everyone I know
Playing mind games on the phone
Beg you to leave me alone
Then ask you to walk me home

I'll get you alone
Then lose my backbone
My mother doubts my moral code
I give myself a pep talk in the mirror for
hours on end
But then in the moment my mind is
spiraling
Here we go again

Then I'll scold myself
Because I swore the bridges had burned
But those flames still hurt
Put the matches on the bottom shelf
In hopes I'd use them more often
But I get caught up in
What-ifs and what-could-have-beens
You said you want to see me again
But I translate that to you hate me
I don't want to look so just tell me when you
leave

You were standing starry-eyed in the
doorway
So why do I feel like I'm in the way?
The kind of silence that feels like safety
Trying to figure out how to get hurt safely
But I'll destroy myself before I let you ruin
me
I should just let it go and let it be
But then everything would be off
And then you actually saw the real me
And all I said was sorry
And you said don't be
You say you want this
But do you want me?

And I try to be more clever and less naive
But I'll push you out then convince myself
you wanted to leave
You could hang the stars and I'd still turn
the lights on
Then I'll wonder why I can't go stargazing
I'm trying to get it wrong
But you're still staying

I'll conspire against myself
Then commit the crime
I don't need anyone's help

Till I'm locked in a cage I welded of my
own volition
Then I'll pick up the phone
Ask you to pay my bail
And you'll ask why
I'll say I was on a mission
Wonder how far you would have driven
Or if you would even come at all
If I picked up the phone and called

The pattern is repeating
We draw on my ceiling
Now I start believing
But if I know better
I know I don't go heroically
I always go kicking and screaming
And everyone's voicemail tells me:
Just relax, you're going to make it through
Your own worst enemy is you

Periphery

I've been tracing footsteps, counting petals
And feeling sorry for myself
Wondering if anyone is going to help

I've been writing letters
To people who don't want to hear from me
And I've been lying to my reflection
Telling her it's going to be getting better
But I turn on my heels and run in the other
direction
And I've been counting down the days
Even though I don't know what they're
leading up to
I think I can feel the water slipping through
the cracks
Or maybe it's just the past
The bandaids stopped sticking to the cuts
I think of calling someone but I don't wanna
make a fuss

Then I notice that line getting bigger in my
periphery
But I won't be satisfied till you leave me
So I'll pack your bag for you and zip it
closed
And then watch you go

Treasure Chest Closed

One day the treasure chest closed
And never opened back up
And in it is locked all the childhood love

Keeping lists of all the boys we've kissed
Secrets we keep and drunkenly share
Bruises from bleachers and first love affairs
Shoes for the bars, a culture so fine tuned
Just for a couple of years the broken glass
glitters like a chandelier
Rooms full of faces and places
What are we doing here?
What are we going to do?

No one cares but everyone is staring
The getting ready is always better than the
party
The high feels cheap but it does it's job
We won't be this young for long

Grew up enough to walk on alone
To a haunted home
Too dumb to let go of the make believe
Used to think love had to be a tangible thing
But cracks in the pavement hold my tears
and broken American dreams

Threads of my sweater stuck on the couches
that belong to people I no longer see
Empty bottles painted and filled with pieces
of memories
Crowds that will never see me again
Strangers who became friends
All the times I watched a good thing end
And everything that has begun
Grew up enough to find the shades of love
Learning people as much as lessons
People who knew me but don't know me
Crying in a bathroom stall over the make
believe
Who am I supposed to be?

Grew up enough to learn the laws
And then break them all on a Thursday
night
Snow falling under purple street lights
Blurry vision and a heart that's missing
people who don't call anymore
People who planned the runaway to a
foreign country
People who know all of me
People who remember everything and know
I can't forget
People who don't know where I am in the
world

People whose birthday passed and I didn't
say a word

People are people and they always die
Even when they're still alive

Smile on my face
Fear of things we can't control
When did we get so old?
I wonder if this feeling will ever replicate
10 years from now, where are we going to
be?

The Final Girl

That list of all the things you've ruined for
me–
You helped me build it, too
Which makes it even more cruel

When you put on your 501 Levi's,
Do you think of the last night we said
goodbye?
I know you saw the hope in my eyes
Did you plan it like a surprise?
But my secret encoded letters in your jacket
pocket
Our memories stay in a locket on a chain
October will never glow the same

I was falling under orange fluorescent lights
Our pinky promise
And one fallen knife
Days in a row
We laughed at the 4am infomercials as they
robbed us
Of good money and decent sleep
I felt myself start to believe in something
good
We talked about what we'd draw on my
bedroom ceiling

A make believe treasure map
Your head on my pillow, I watched as you
were dreaming
And I started believing
But all kingdoms reign wild then collapse

You were shiny in the Sunday morning light
But the closer I looked you were just tin foil
But I did it, I took the chance
I knew this was going to make a mess of me
Either ashes or confetti

Standing red cheeked in the doorway
Why'd you look at me with crescent moon
eyes,
While mine were full star galaxies?
Going through the motions
Of ill fated last goodbye formalities

I was explaining the artwork in my room
You said no one makes you laugh like I do
All our friends were rooting for us too
You painted me golden over the burning red
For once I wasn't reading just to get to the
end
But even a part of the final girl always ends
up dead

You told me I should write in permanent ink
Stop writing my dreams in pencil
You always wanted to know what I thought
you'd think about everything
And I'm far too sentimental
But with you nothing was ever confidential
And I liked that
Now it's 5am and we're roller coasting
through my imagination
Stargazing, charting out all the
constellations
In the right neck of the woods heading in the
right direction
But daylight illumination
Gave way to graveyard shift bullshit
I guess I'll add you to my collection
Of broken mosaic unasked questions
And here we are at 2am
Doe-eyed at the top of the world
Was too naive to know then
I was the final girl

All of it can be true
I believed what I wanted to
But you swore this time I wouldn't lose
And so I believed you
The artifacts of long gone loves withered in
receding shivers

Stare at the wounded reflection in the
mirror
Cut all the loose threads with rusty scissors
Almost recognized the killer
Now all my midnights crease like pages of a
book half read
A part of the final girl always ends up dead

I replay the highlight reel
When we were falling right into each other
All the missteps
You were hiding in plain sight
Perfectly undercover
You never looked like a suspect
But standing in a line up I guess you really
do look like the rest
But I swear I tried my best

I stumble through the reeling
Curse myself for believing
The violent heart to heart
Almost at the end
The sharpest blades cut the deepest
Sometimes you don't even feel it
Till even your bones are bleeding
I stayed hopeful till the end

The jury has mixed thoughts

Some say it was a clean break
Others say it is all alleged
But no one really thought you'd get caught
Red handed fingerprints on my body that
you held close
Why'd you do it? No one truly knows

My best friend saw you at my funeral
I knew you'd attend
Because no matter how hard she tries
The final girl always ends up dead

As Far As Landslides Go

We were tangled up together
Lips and limbs
The morning light was dim
There was an ache in my chest I addressed
as daylight
But it introduced itself instead as something
much more grim
Some sort of foreign language I'd heard
only in passing
I couldn't quite translate it
But I knew I'd be fluent in it soon

All the best lessons sit on the shelf
Like participation trophies
It just hurts like hell
What's the point in trying just for silver?
You only get the credit when you're the
winner

My mother told me as far as landslides go
You were the best one I had known
But I was stubborn and relentless

Mid October crossing paths with a gray
Friday afternoon
I told my mother I didn't need her right now

Because I didn't have any open wounds
Did you take that as a challenge,
Or just a promise to break in half?

It was simple and quite painless overall
But I'm not familiar with the protocol
For something that isn't a wreckage
If you just give me a second
I could tell you I'm fine
But I'm stubborn, relentless, and dramatic
Patching up my scratches after you left was
somehow automatic
Like I knew how to do it all along
Like I got to decide if the ghost of you got to
haunt

There's raindrops on your jacket hanging in
my apartment
There's a pile of your things you left here
that you'll never get back
I cut up your socks like I was an artist
Then threw them out the window into the
November pitch black

There's no anger that I reside in
There's confetti on the pillows on my bed
And there's ashes for the bridges with you
that stay burned

Some sort of foreign language that told me
it's okay if the lesson is learned
And the part of my heart that belongs to you
no longer hurts

Tourist

Did your heart skip a beat when you walked
past me?
Did you think about the excitement and then
the come down?
Were you sorry in the moment,
Or did you know it from the moment you
knocked on my door?
When we walked downtown at midnight
The October streetlights on brick roads
looked so pretty
Feeling like a tourist in this city

I've rearranged my apartment since you've
been here last
But I can't sit on my couch
It's a little too on the nose
That actor from our favorite show
Won an award for his performance
To think you left without any warning
I saw you downtown yesterday
I think I saw something in your eyes
Or maybe it was a flashback memory
To when you told me I'd never watch you
leave

The irony was that café

Where the waitress had to kick us out
Because the line was out the door and all the
tables were full
I remember thinking then I'd probably never
eat here again
This place would always remind me of you
Did you ever think about that day?
When we walked by it going our separate
ways
That café witnessed new beginnings and
fresh starts
And yesterday it witnessed
Two tangled souls
And an old flame's dying sparks

At the corner of the crossroads
When you left it broke my bones
Snowy boots on cobblestones
Couldn't change the truth
We were strangers fitting in
Like there was nothing happening
Like we couldn't read between the lines
Like I knew you well enough
To perfectly lose my mind
It happened way too quickly
I try to keep myself busy
Like a tourist in this city

A Midwest moon
Some sirens in the background
Footsteps in my kitchen
You spoke to me in cursive
You are one of my top 3 favorite verses
My friends talked about the curse and
You laughed at the movie trailer and the
music video
It was only for a visit but you really felt like
home

I'm the best time you had
And the one good thing you'll never have

I got rid of your souvenirs
Thought you bought them from the gift
shop
But you were just a pickpocket
Now it's winter here
Snowflakes in my eyebrows
The slow come down from your letdown
Are you sorry?
Or are you sorry it was a cop out?
I thought you were picturesque
But you were evidently just like the rest
I thought you'd complete me
But you were just a tourist in this city

The 12th floor window has our fingerprints
From when we pointed out our favorite trees
And then we kissed
The cracks in the sidewalk and the floorboards
Are you sorry?
I think you thought it could work out
But this city was more than you wanted to afford
So you had cut your trip short
The worst way to walk home after a high is alone

Do you miss the 4am memories?
The photographs?
The things you lost that you will never get back?
I was high on exploration
And the promise that you were staying

The Good One

I think I tried my best to forget
Act like it was for the time being
You came into my life unexpectedly
I was finally believing
But you pinky promised I'd never be
watching you leaving
You were the best

But I won't forget you
Did you think I would?
No matter how far away I run
You'll always be the good one

It was ethereal inside my head
Dreaming side by side in my bed
My diary sitting on my desk
You read and lived for every word I said
Flannels and Carharrt litter my heart
And maybe I was misled
Now all I do is think about the start
And when everything just stopped

I miss you when the lights flicker shadows
on my couch
I miss you when I'm walking by our favorite
spots downtown

I miss you when the music gets too loud
I miss you when I turn the sheets down
I miss you just when I think I've forgotten
you
And I think I'm finally done
But I can't forget the good one

I see you out everywhere
Then it hits me that I still care
It was an autumn affair
An answered prayer
The formers never compared

But when you stopped me on the street just
to say hi
You undid goodbye
I started to ask you why
But followed up suit
You said it was good to see me
And I said you too
I saw it in your eyes
I wondered on my whole walk home if you
forgot it all
I wondered if you'd pick your phone up and
call

Why did seeing you feel like a hit and run?

There's nothing bad, there was no brutal
war
Just echoes of you walking out my door
I wish I could hate you
But I wish you'd come back more
You handled it all with such care
Now I just sit feeling bare
I wish I could thank you for cleaning up the
glass after you broke it
You were the best, and I hope you know it
You're second best to none
You'll always be the good one

Swimming Pool Shark

I feel like I'm going to run into you around
every corner
Think I see you even when you aren't there
I finally took off all my armor
Thinking I was floating in warmer waters
But you emerged from the deep blue
Let me believe I really had you

Now it's too scary to scrape the bottom
Think it's becoming a big problem
How I'm still in the deep end
And you've already forgotten last autumn

Now you drift by me
All the way out, 6 feet deep
I'll find a way to swim again
An imagination foe and friend

And I'm superstitious you were always
there
I curse you for always being there
Big teeth, big dreams, even bigger fears

Shout your name like I'm a little kid
It's just my mind playing tricks

Now I'm drowning my other body parts
Drinking till the tide restarts
How far can you swim?
Lose sight of the edge
I can't make it make sense

You were there, I swam with you
You were there, weren't you?

I think I see you and it's true
Broken heart stained chlorine blue
Wade out into the truth
You'd never stay forever
You just scared me into believing it's so
Still I stayed tempting fate
Great whites hide below
Maybe I should have known

I haven't been able to sleep at night
Think I see your face in every shadow
thrown by light
Looking for you in the darkest places
But I overfill my emptiest spaces
You're just hiding inside my mind
If I was a better swimmer I might have been
alright

And if the wound didn't hurt in the moment

I'd bleed out till I picked up the phone and
Realized there was no one to call to drown it
all out
Just a stone and a sock to throw
Down to the bottom
Treading water trying to spot him
Superficial teeth marks on my heart
From the swimming pool shark

Gold Star

You're swimming circles in my mind like a
fish
The justification of just one kiss
Peter said, *"Wendy, close your eyes and
believe in this"*
Sharing secrets across the kitchen counter
top
You made little promises in passing jokes
We kept a list of each others funny quotes

You in your t-shirt from Cape Cod
I hate to have the thought
You swim in my currents
But this story, I've heard it

Windows down
On obedient cues
Post tornado sky blue
You listen to me, I fall into you

Your greatest misstep was never refusing to
growing up
It was thinking I'd forgive you in the blink
of an eye
But I'll never forget enough
And I'll remember it till the day I die

And when I opened up it closed you off
It had been a couple months since I felt
something this soft

You held out your hand
But it was too good to be true
Wendy left everything behind just on the
premise of believing in you
You promised the world but all you gave
was Neverland
Wendy loved the boy who would never be
the man

Lost Boys are always running away from
time
Shooting stars are hard to find
But I stayed all night
And you were just the twist of the knife

You didn't have to break me that hard
Here's your gold star
You knew my weakness
But I was never going to give in and give it
up
You knew for me it had to be love
So you had to run

We were never going to grow up the way the
other needed
To think I almost conceded
We visited Neverland for different reasons

I don't know if I'll forgive you for making
the time of my life a waste of my time
But that's the hoax when it comes to aging
If I'd never seen the second star from the
right
Straight on till morning
I'd never have known how big the sky is
I'd still be collecting gold stars
Peter would get so bored
Wendy would be stuck forever just waiting

It's a tale as old as the galaxies themselves
And as young as the girl he puts up on the
shelf
Tinkers with her youth and twists her to give
in
And she almost did
It's a tale as old as Two Cities
And as young as she is pretty

Wendy left Peter checking in with the
window pane
She's already a world away

Peter missed his chance to be a grown up
His gold star was never enough
Wendy twirled in her nightgown
Looked up at the sky, stuck on the ground
She closed the curtains and stopped looking
out
Wendy was charmed by Peter's
winsomeness
But all she wanted was to keep was her
innocence
And so she did

Holiday

I'll follow you
Till my feet run bare
And my hope has gone scarce
Even after all your disregard
I'd still send you postcards
That's another bag packed
In the name of broken halves
And thrown punches missed and ricocheted
How do I get back all that I gave?
Even if we're worlds away
We're still looking at the same stars
I hope you read my postcards

Standing outside the hotel, was it everything
you dreamed?
Are you proud you kept it clean?
The memories are good but never good
enough
I don't know why I keep them
What was I high on?
I'll look for you on your birthday
And you'll say you were wrong for walking
away
And I'll say all these other cities are special
in their own way
But you're my favorite holiday

I need to understand why the sun rises in the
east and sets in the west
I bury the hatchet and I try to forget
But up in the high rise
Fingerprints on the window pane
I'll always remember our holiday
And I don't understand the opposites in the
hemispheres
When outside the hotel I asked you what
you were doing here
I think you almost invited me in to stay
I wish I could understand why we shared a
bed
Nestled in blanket forts hiding from all the
things left unsaid
As if the gray area didn't matter if we
traveled to the edge of my world
But the train had one last stop to make
I was in it for the long haul
But I was just your holiday

And now I search for your face in strangers
What if I look for you for the rest of my
life?
You knew what you were doing when you
had me explain the album that became your
namesake

When you held my hand and told me not to
worry
So I didn't, I was brave
But then you left in a hurry
The words were true but now it's a shame

What if I don't forgive you for speaking my
name?
What if the postcards never deliver?
And you forget my reflection in the mirror
When we watched the sun come up
The sky was blushed and it felt like hope
But it was just the numb from my broken
bones you put in a cast
But now how do I get my city back?

I keep waiting for you to come back
Now the holiday is all we have
And I sunk so fast
But I knew you were hooked when you
dropped me off to meet my mom
Now even she thinks of you when she hears
our song

Safe travels back to the place from which
you came
You can't stop me now, I'm already on my
plane

But if you tried I might forgive you all the
same
Because all these other cities are special in
their own way
But you're still my favorite holiday

Yet, the passport stamp stained jet black
And I'm on my way to take my city back

Mountain Peaks

I think you got closest to my mountain peaks
And I got really good at hiking
You got really good at tracing my outline on
the bed sheets

The world is too wide
I shouldn't know exactly where you are
tonight
I can see it all
The way your night played out
You were drinking beer for cheap
downtown
And suddenly we speak now

You're sitting at the dive bar
I know you're still thinking
And you know I'm still dreaming
You put on your brave face but it's just little
old me
The tangled knot tying us together with a
softness that belonged
We always could caress each other's heart
strings

You walked out of the outlet mall

The summer bugs in your windshield
watched you feel guilty
I can see it all
The notification and all the time you spent
waiting on yourself
If you weren't in a rush that day then maybe
we could have talked more outside the hotel
You said you're glad I'm doing well

You were being genuine
I was done with skeletons
Till you opened up that door and came
rushing back in
And I'd still do it all again
The past is the past but this is right now
And we're just two tourists who can't put
the others' postcards down

The causality of forgiveness is that you
never forget
It's summer now and you ask me how I'm
doing
I touch my fingertips and still feel your
silhouette
It's summer now and I tell you where I'm
going
And the clock keeps ticking forward in time

Knowing the two hearts might be sorry, but
right now isn't right

But you were still trying to work out how
this could ever work
Knowing you missed the mark
And I missed the way you held my heart in
your strong hands
I heard the autumn air is colder across the
Atlantic Ocean
But I had to spread my wings and make my
own plans
I had to make peace with your notions

And you know it too
I'm going to spend forever hiking on trails
that lead me back to you

But I know it best believe
You're going to spend forever hiking on
trails that lead you back to me

Maybe 6 months from now we'll both be in
the right place
I'll meet you outside our café
We can talk for hours like we always used to
We can sit in the dark again
Your arm around my shoulder

We can talk about the music and the weight
of getting older
We can hike to the very top of our mountain
peaks
And this time it will be right
And we will never have to leave

The Rabbit Hole

Really in it Now

Well, here we are now
I don't know you
But I'd like to find out
Heard you're from my state
Now we can talk
And I'll gaze at your face

I keep up
With your footsteps everywhere
My head screaming at me
That this could be tragic
But I don't even care
I've got to have it

Oh no, I'm totally all in this
And we haven't even kissed
I think I'm really in it now
It might even be reckless
But I'm so committed
Worried that you'll turn me down
But our chemistry is so infectious

And I don't even think that it would be wise
Told my friends that you're just some guy
But you got me just overnight
And I'm talking to you but just in my mind

Maybe we could be right

I'm just outside
If you want to meet up
It's brand new
But I think it could be love

And I got you in the blink of an eye
Us at the coffee shop on a Thursday night
Yeah it feels so right
We talked about president assassinations
Oh my god we have a situation
Feeling so intoxicated by you

And I said I didn't feel it but that wasn't the
truth
Think I'm really down bad and into you
I think maybe you feel it too

And here we are now in the middle of a
crowd
You hold my hand and the world drowns
out
Think we're both really in it now

Outlaw

Sharing secrets through our fingertips
Hand on the bottle, you're at the top of my
list
I know that I should look somewhere else
I should turn you in instead of myself

But with you there's no reason to be
someone else
Carving initials on empty bottles
A secret affair that will just collect dust on
your shelf
The truth comes out when we reach the
bottom

You knew what you were doing
Your finger on a freshly polished trigger
And you gave it right back to me
We were both fatalists
Who's eyes said things they couldn't admit

A Monday afternoon we went to the shops
To buy costumes for Halloween
Whoever finds the cowboy hat first gets to
play for keeps
And I found the hat first but we both went to
my roommates' party dressed the same

Strayed from the plan, came as no shock

Took one of my favorite pictures of you that
day
Standing in front of the city sign to
commemorate

You'll be my outlaw
We're sharing a cowboy hat
And acting like we aren't the best thing that
we've both had
I'll be your biggest loss
We're sharing everything we have
And acting like we won't miss each other so
bad
When the moments gone
You'll be my outlaw

I'd come find you in a dust storm
I'm the holster keeping your gun warm
If you shoot I'd die
Just to come along for the ride

I know everywhere you hide
Maybe it's just the dust in my eyes
But I think you love me tonight

When the lights went up and I got caught

There I was white knuckled behind bars
You visited one last time
You said true love is hard
And it's better if I leave you lost
Everything I wanted was hung on a sign
I paid for all your crimes
We're sharing a cowboy hat
And dreams of each other that we shouldn't
have
So you'll ride out of my town leaving
nothing but a cloud of smoke
Leaving me with our cowboy hat
And a solo curtain call for the pony show

Clean Cut

You rolled your sleeves up as I undid the
buttons on your shirt
You pulled my face in and said I'm a
mastermind
I knew it worked
I got nearly everything I wanted
Now my temporary home is haunted
I said you really look like you're from
Chicago
Now your footsteps are all I follow
It's a clean cut any way you cut it
You're going to return to the city and I'll
just be hollow

That thing you'd be taking from me,
You'd be giving me something too
Because I chose you
So I put myself in the man's shoes
And in the man's sheets

Said you want to get married at 29
To a girl you've known your whole life
You proposed to me in bed and I said fine
You were only joking, but I could be your
wife

I'm throwing my life away
And I see it happening but I don't know how
to stop it
You scrolled through the playlists
Pinned me down with a laugh and a cheek
kiss
Planned out the final goodbye
I wasn't asking for a lot
I just didn't want a temporary high

When you kissed my mouth you bit my
tongue
That was the only way to shut me up
I can't believe I believed you
So now we're not hugging at the pub like we
used to
And my master plan fell through

I wasn't okay with how it all went down
When I heard you were in Paris
I almost said something
But I couldn't bear it
It was a clean cut
It was coming from a mile away
But it still felt so abrupt

Orchard Road

Cross my heart and I hope it's a lie
I'll never walk down Orchard Road again
At least not in this life

From coffee afternoons
To blooming sunrises
Our secret language in a stranger-littered
room
Save my meanest jokes to tell to you
You know all my disguises
Every version of me in the palm of your
hand
Ready to be held and crushed
In the violent name of trust

We run through the rain past the bus station
We talked about if we were staying
What life would look like then
There with the moonlight through the blinds
You said I'm your best friend
And after all this time
I feel safe again

You fall asleep in the passenger seat of the
taxi
I watch the lights flash across your skin

All I want is for you to be happy
Then we walk down the street to the little
bar in the bricks
We talk about spiders and how you always
have to win
Down an alleyway past the mural of a fish
Cutting through the restaurant patio
Drunk eyes in an empyrean haze
All around the world,
From right here back to Orchard Road

With cigarettes at 3am
And conversations that never end
Drunken confessions and safety nets
Saying we'd hate life if we never met
Eating Chinese takeout on my bedroom
floor
Drinking cheap wine as I explain my
favorite songs on 'evermore'
The secrets shared under warm lamp light
Laughing at the restaurant every Sunday
night
Our footsteps in sync on uneven pavement
With a tequila smile you said I'm your
favorite
Push and pull this thread of gold
We'll always have Orchard Road

Do You Want to Run Away?

I'll have to readapt
In seventeen days

If I asked you to run away
Would you do it?

It was good to know you
Even just for a short time
You know there's nothing I wouldn't do
To see you again in another life

You're worried about your brother
You secretly miss your mother
You talk about your father
He's why you learned to whisper
He's why you became a shapeshifter

You're worried about Christmas
Said you're going to miss this
Opened up just enough to know you're
scared
You are being brave
You said with me you feel safe

You came out of the darkest blue
What will I ever do without you?

There's so much I never knew
Till I saw the world through your eyes
Walking away will be the worst of all time
Staying up with you till the sun rose
Memorize the sound of all our best nights
I'll love you wherever I go

You talk about who you were
And who you want to be
We share all of our thoughts
You know how my brain operates
I know what you're about to say
I talk about feeling small in the world
Show each other all the parts of ourselves
we once tried to burn

I know all of your countermoves
I've never been this close to someone
What am I ever going to do?

I'll love you till the sights to see become
nothing
But I still show up anyway
Because you'll always be worth loving
Even when all the colors fade to gray

This will be the hardest goodbye
I don't how I'll re-adjust

On the comedown from the greatest high
Don't know if there's anyone else we will
ever trust

There's a million places calling our names
I think we should just do it now
Do you want to run away?

The Truth Is

The truth is you blurred the lines
Said you didn't think about the end of time
But you brought it up first

Was it worth all the bruises?
And every single one of our truces
Were just a bandaid over what you couldn't
escape
Did you like me better when I took the
blame?
When I defended you to everyone we know
The truth is it was heartless
But I still wouldn't go

Did you despise me because I held up the
mirror?
Or because you missed me when you were
with her?
Did I deserve to play pretend?
You got your walk away
You had a savior complex
And cigarettes in your pockets
The truth is in me you found solace

If you just said the word, I'd never leave

You taught me the language then forgot how
to speak when I needed you most
When I fell asleep wearing your jacket
The truth is I should have left that night, I
know
But you gave me hope
The truth is you knew exactly what you
were doing
And I think I could kill you but I'd rather be
the one bruising

The truth is the words you spoke in the dark
were the truth
Did you think I was a doll in a toy house?
I should hate you for everything
But I'm not even close
I'd rather hold you than hold a grudge
All I ever think about is if it was love
I think if it wasn't I could throw a punch

The truth is I cut you open
I think I wasted my breath tip toeing
You believed that if your eyes were shut
then you wouldn't see it
But you had me from the jump
The truth is all I ever think about is if it was
love

So I'll pretend that I'm looking for cars
when I cross the street
But the truth is I'm looking for you
Even if it kills me

Shoot First

You left your lighter in my room
Just to start a fire overnight
I got so close to you
At the speed of light
Then it all fell through
You pulled the trigger out of spite
For the man you'd never be
I thought I was bullet proof
Or maybe I thought you'd never shoot me

I called you a fucking liar
Hoping that it'd hit
I said *"I love you"*
And you didn't even flinch

You called me for who I am
But you couldn't call it what it was
You'd rather die than give a damn
And I'd rather die than admit you weren't in love

Taylor

The girl with her hair in a bow
Will search for him wherever she goes
She memorized his every move when they
we're together
And she smiled because she always knew
better
But she held out hope
Taylor always knows
Taylor told her so

She tries to bleed pastel pink but it's always
bright burning red
She's wearing his hoodie knowing come
morning she'll never see him again
He didn't understand Taylor so he didn't
understand her
With her vibrant optimism and reckless
hope
He kissed her forehead and didn't mean the
words he spoke
She made the playlist she prayed she'd
never have to use
Her mother said "*he wasn't the one*"
That was the honest to god truth

He pulled her close, wrapped her in warmth

Said he'd see her later
And she had been warned
If only she listened to Taylor

He said she's a mastermind
She thought it was the right time
And he listened to all the songs
She tried to forget what could have been
She should have listened to Taylor instead

He wanted the deep blue sea
Dreamed of being a sailor
While she dreamed of being Taylor

The Weather App

I've got your new city in my weather app
Just to check it every now and then
For old times sake
How is Spain?

I'll go back to all the things I once knew
And every day you said you missed me too
But the distance between us was going up in
smoke
I always knew it in my bones

I dug my nails in and tore the skin
Hoping to keep things how they've been
My bloody knuckles in your steady palms
Why does forgetting last so long?
I won't ever forget a thing
Do you still miss me?

Everything I know
Is turning to dust on Orchard Road
Now you're somewhere on a beach
There are words I won't forget
I know you meant it when you said
You're really glad that our paths crossed
You said I should come visit you in Spain
I could work out a way

Even if it killed me

When we hugged goodbye you lingered in
my doorway
I was dreaming of showing you around
Broadway
I said *"I'm here for you, always"*

When you left, you didn't look back
The depraved thing is I expected that
But I'll always look at the weather app

The Archeologist

The night we met you asked me if I believed
in God
Then I told you my every thought
You laughed with your head back when I
said I wanted to dye my hair blonde
At the picnic table you smoked a cigarette
Watched my every move
You were wearing black and navy blue
You were already a bruise
But I never felt more calm

Autumn felt like looking forward to
tomorrow
Nothing mattered more than you and me on
the third floor
Talking about things out of our control
And childhood memories that haunt us like
bed sheet covered ghosts
Sharing a bottle and the isolation of feeling
hollow

I'd make my bed and fold my laundry
You'd sit at my desk and just watch me
I held my knees close with my back against
the wall

You played with a pile of spare change and
I'd watch the coins fall

All the things you buried made it hard for
you to breathe
I was the fresh air in your lungs
But you smoked too often to fully come
clean

You said I know you better
Than anyone ever has before
I unearthed your skeletons
You told me I helped you through the worst
of it
I said *"I love you"* again
For good measure
But you weren't listening

You're in my bones, you're in my veins,
you're in all my secrets
You're on the tip of my tongue even when
I'm not speaking
I'm only half of myself but it's like I
stopped breathing
Without you around

You'd throw me a bone that was broken
But I'd take anything as a compliment

You'd always give me something I could up
and run with

Three months later you keep me buried
under city lights and your new address
Now I'm a quiet suburb American dream
A new postal code with new things to say

Where'd you go?
Who'd you run into running away from me?
If you went back to keeping secrets
I don't want to know anything

I'm not an archeologist
I surrender digging you up
I'm just an optimist
Who hoped you'd call it love

Cheetah in a Cage

You were like a cheetah in a cage
First glance of freedom you were bound to
run away
But you always licked all my bones clean
Think you were starving for intimacy
We were naked time and time again
Without ever removing anything

Does the shirt I gave you have holes in it
yet?
Is it worn in or have you worn it out ?

You told me all the lines you'd never cross
and then you did anyways
We were both fools
I thought you'd stay
And you thought I'd stay away

It was colder that day at the zoo than either
of us expected
Our heads were crowded with pulses from
the night before
There was little to no chance we'd ever
make it out alive
The sign on the cage was rusted over but it
said 'THESE ANIMALS MAY BITE'

It was right

I'm sorry that your past made you cruel
And that all my goodness couldn't wash it
out of you
You think love and violence are the same
thing
So you always bite the hand that feeds

Fake Our Deaths

There in front of the convenience store
We talked about life after leaving Cork
We daydreamed about the hotel lobby across
the street
Decorated with golden lights and a
Christmas tree

You smoked two cigarettes
We shared a bag of crisps
Saying how much we're going to miss this
Running around and running away
We could fake our deaths

We missed the last call for the train
Sitting on the bench as the starlings circled
the late afternoon sky
Making a plan for our never ending night
Standing room only on the train
We hid in plain sight
Then we snuck our way through the station
We never bought the 2 euro tickets
You looked back at me with a toothy smile
when they let us in
We were criminals who'd always flee the
scene
We never needed more than this

Our last dinner
Breaking chopsticks across the table from
me
You waited for me to eat
I know all of your top secret identities
I know exactly the man you want to be

I should have smoked a cigarette with you
when I had the chance
And I had so many chances
But we were always on something else
Something that not even your dealer dealt
It was something bigger than us
Read somewhere that they call it love

We had places we'd hideout
You got me to watch horror films
I got you to learn all the Taylor albums
That was a crime unto itself
Your dad's book you kept on the top shelf
Told me you never read it, but you might
I'd already written your eulogy
Even though you'd never felt more alive
Put it in the box of your things I kept on my
desk
I asked you if you had read it and you said
"not yet"

I didn't know it then
But it was a death sentence

I wanted to but I couldn't believe you
When you told me you'd find me in all your
past lives
Even in this one we didn't have enough
time
You wanted to but you didn't understand
When I told you I knew from the moment
you held my hand

And there in the greenhouse surrounded by
butterflies
I knew I'd be missing you my whole life

Bird on the Wire

When you told me you'd walk me the hour
home
At 2am when I bought you water as the store
was about to close
You shouted into the night how much you
care about me
I danced off the curb and spun in the street
You didn't look both ways before you
jumped in
I wanted it to always be like this

Your desperate pleas and laughs on that
walk home
Talking to the chirping bird on the wire
A car passed us by going over the limit
The world was wide but we were the only
people in it
Your laugh echoed over the pathway
You told me if I wasn't leaving, you would
have stayed
In the heat of the moment I called you a liar
But I was smiling, burning in the fire

For all the heights you were scared of I was
your vertigo

I was your escape from all the places you
didn't want to go
And problems you didn't want to face
I was your treehouse where you could hide
out
And not take any of the blame
I know I'm going to forgive you
As if it's all the same

We were worth our weight in gold
This city's brightest firework show

You told me that you loved me but never to
my face
It was something you could never bring
yourself to say
I looked for it in all the punctuation
When we sat on the floor and you started
playing 'reputation'
I grabbed your lighter and lit the flame
You grabbed my hand and took it away
Said you don't want to see me hurt
But that day at the movie you wore the shirt
I gave to you in future memoriam
Said I remind you of something Victorian
And we talked about all our past lives we
said we'd find each other in

You told me all the things you never say out
loud
Like why you think you've let your father
down
Why you sometimes have to sleep with
sound

I told you why I don't believe in myself
most of the time
Why I make people my lifelines
Why I ruin myself every time

We broke the rules and got lost in it

We were each other's faith
We pushed pins in all our favorite places
You told me I could do what I wanted with
my life
I told you about what keeps me up at night
You were the safety of leaving on a light
All those times I got you to dance with a
smile on your face
It was bittersweet on that last Sunday
We almost did it, we almost ran away
There were stories of lost us in wonderland
Talking in a language only we could
understand
The only witness was the bird on the wire

Everyone else was just an outsider

When you asked me to come to your
apartment
Because you felt safer with me there
Then when I said "*I love you*"
You just stared
Like I was the chirping bird on the wire
Out of place to your ear
But this is it
I loved you here

Better You

Heard from our friend you're happier in
your new city
The one you wouldn't be in if I didn't leave
Is it everything you dreamed?
Was it worth more than what you had to
lose?
I know you better
But just between us, are you a better you?

I asked you how you're doing now
And didn't push back when you lied to my
face
Whoever you are now, it's not true
I guess you have a better view in your new
place
Back in February you were still being
honest
When you told me you didn't want it to be
like this
But you were soul searching for something
you already found in me
And this is how I found out:

You told our friend you took a flight to
Amsterdam just to kiss your ex

Then you made sure I heard about it just to
mess with my head
Do you really think you're better off saying
you never meant a word you said?
You lied to me about that trip
Since I'm not around anymore, how locked
is your crypt?

Oh so you say you don't feel bad
It's just a front
One wrong thing, you need my help
Then suddenly we're not done
You started it
You didn't back down
Then you got hurt when I wrote you out
Push me out, pull me back in
See you in Dublin, never see you again
Get it twisted and then you don't
You blame me for the words you spoke

You say you're better off and I hope that's
true
But we both know you're not a better you

Start a War

I'd start a war for you
I think I already did
I think you might be happy
I know I should just let you live
I'm thinking about all the times before
I didn't know a thing
I'm not the strongest soldier
But you made me believe
I saw you're doing well
You're wearing the same old shoes
Do you forget the things you felt?
Did someone else come out of the blue?
If it's not me, who are you turning toward?
Is she everything you need?
For you I'd start a war

You started smoking cigarettes in July
Your host mom gave you a 3 months supply
You didn't like who you were when you met
me
I told you I'd love you in all your bitter
glory

If we were just a false god,
Does she know why you're scared of the
dark?

The fake flowers I gave you push pinned on
your wall
I teased you about playing golf
The poster I gave you that you taped up
poorly
So it fell down that night
The same night you said with me your life is
never boring

I'd start a war over that night with the rain
Sitting on the floor with bad red wine
Arguing over what T.S Elliot wrote
We stumbled down to the back lot so you
could smoke
There was so much time to say it but I never
spoke
Till it was nearly going, going, gone
I'm pretty sure you wiped the tears from my
face
And I'm pretty sure you meant it when you
said you wanted to stay
In that room through the frost and the heat
You were looking for a reason to never leave

We made a sidewalk chalk plan to meet
again someday
But the December rainstorm came and
washed it away

I stayed on the front lines of storm watch
Because what else was I supposed to do?
I'd start a war for you

Camelot

You were so happy that day walking in
You kept your word, wearing the shirt I
gifted you
I memorized your laugh as we walked down
the street to catch the taxi
Our clothes touching in the backseat
Teased me throughout the whole movie
You said, *"she's not actually playing the
guitar"*
I laughed and shoved your arm
You sang all the songs you knew the words
to
It was something to see and I saw it how I
always knew it
You said I'm your favorite person and the
truth is
All our strings were intertwined
With me you'd always think out loud, great
minds
We were collateral, never one without the
other

At the end of the night we walked ourselves
home
I said with you I never feel alone
Think I tripped on the stairs up

Back in my room we left the light off
Told you why I think I have bad luck
The silver from the full moon was soft
Think that was the night you first said it
It was everything we both needed for so
long
Life was good for us in Camelot

Now I've been keeping track of days and
overthinking
Waking up restless at 5 am
Can't even turn to drinking
Dying isn't the same without my best friend

I've been growing taller
Still hoping you can see me
I hope you feel more free now
I still love you like it's breathing

Now it's the downfall of something once
golden and true
I'm just holding out till June
Tonight is supposed to be a full moon
Same position in the sky as that Saturday in
October
I replay it in my mind over and over

Now I'll be your gray space taking up too
much of your spare time
And you'll be my box of crayons I use to
color my whole life

I hope you look back on it with the warmth
you once had
Chances are I'll always try to go back

The Middle Man

We're dividing up assets and sections of our
minds
I'll keep your fears and you'll keep my time
I'll put on a brave face and scan the eyes I
once knew

We had to use a middle man
As if we didn't just smile and shake our
hands
In the age of you I did so much growing up
So why now do I feel so stuck?

The middle man told me what you said on
the phone
He told me you were drunk but not alone
I couldn't help but wonder about the bar you
were in
And if the new girl you're with meets all
your cynical needs
But I guess if she was that good then you
wouldn't be wondering about me

I told the middle man I will always know
you
But I'm not learning you anymore

I couldn't decide which felt like the deeper
cut
All those fish bowl evenings we spent
together
Where no detail was spared
Nothing has since compared

You told the middle man it was an
exorbitant affair
Something you were grateful for
But you felt like you'd been caught in a
snare
I wasn't some huntsman luring you to your
death
You think true love is a scheme people buy
into just to feel something
Which is why you do drugs instead

At the courthouse on the beach
You drank boxed wine and talked shit about
me
Hand on the Bible, you were lying to the
middle man
About all the ways you've reframed us
In your new plot line, claim you were never
in a trance
And that you never participated in a single
thing since that night you held my hand

The last I heard you were out at some club
I can't even begin to imagine the drugs
And if you are content now
With your feet in the Mediterranean sand
Are you done putting our friends in the
middle?
They can't keep being judicial

I told the middle man they are finally off the
hook
Because I'll always want to but I'll never go
back
I'll just wonder if you like this book

Dog-Eared

I don't think I'll forget you but I will try my
best
I'll read about forgiveness but I'll never lay
it to rest
What does that make me?
What if it's in the clouds and in the smoke?
What if it never goes,
And the story never disappears?
I've tried to let it go but your page is dog-
eared

I hope one day you look back and I hope one
day I don't
I hope one day you're doing well
And I hope there comes a day where I won't
want to know

Never Cold

I was never cold
On all those walks home
And on those walks to all the places we had
to go together
I was never cold
On the cobblestones
Where we'd flirt and fight for worse and for
better

We were always toeing the line
Between *never talk again* and *always be
mine*
It was a lawless state of life
But it was treachery and a never ending
high

You're looking over your shoulder with a
smile at me
A hundred things just said but no one sees
You're ready to laugh the night off on our
walk home
It's pouring rain and we're numbingly cold
But it doesn't matter at all
A wildfire we keep feeding and tending to
every waking minute

You throw your hands in the air
enthusiastically
We're burning up no matter which way you
spin it

We left the house party early so we could go
get food
Watched the goldfish in the tank
We had never been more amused
In the quiet of the 11pm no rush
We kept the restaurant open as we slinked
across the street
To sit on the steps in a fiery blush

I cracked your code, which is why with me
you were never cold
You got my password, which is why the
frostbite was the worst

You gave me your lighter and I burnt our
fingers
The same ones we had the other wrapped
around
That feeling lingered
Even though it was in the the middle of a
thunderstorm
We were living on a cloud

In This Life

All your dark places you worked so hard to
bury deep
I know I came along and unearthed hard
things

I hope you think of me when that song
comes up on your playlist
You showed me on the plane that you were
listening to it
I felt my stomach twist
I let you in
So I'll drink to this

I cut you in half
You cut me deep
I was your cigarette ash
You were the language I speak

I think about all the ways you've ruined me
And how I let that slide
But I wanted it
I wanted it in this life

Default

I got high in the Blue Ridge Mountains
I took the drugs to be anywhere else in the
galaxy
Waltzed away from reality
And the poems collect dust by the hundreds
Muscle memory, I look for you in the haze
I've got a list of things I want to say
But only the trees and the dogs on the porch
are listening to me

I ignore the lighter that isn't yours
And the fact that I smoked without you
After I swore my fear of highs would be
broken with you
Maybe in a parallel universe I didn't always
make a cliche literature joke about
cigarettes
But we played out the same scene every
time
Lit under fluorescents our silhouettes
Stood eye to eye
But one looked away as the other cried
A broken clock is right eventually
I knew you loved me but you'd always want
to leave

Knowing you, you don't talk about your
past
Deflect to something on the table when they
ask
You said you really missed talking life
through with me
But then you turned on a dime, told me lies
I'm begging the middle man to recite the
conversation you two had
So maybe I could revive something torn in
half

Your hieroglyphs of broken dreams
Pictures that I'll never see
Of your new smile
Our splintered table that we once shared
A gloomy season of desperate prayers
An inimitable high, a coordinate cross
Once in a life, a poignant loss

Your self-appointed halo
Your fall from grace
Your glass house
Stones thrown with my name
Your quick change at your new curtain call
A brand new outlook and all your settings
reprogrammed back to default

All your take back words and burning files
Once as true to each other as a sundial
But all those days of wild and shelter
Boiled down to my one letter
A confessional, a heart on a sleeve
A pep talk before the fatality
Your cynical smile, my lonesome heart
The final glance stood no chance
Against the fact that you wanted the comfort
of me in the dark
But you wanted the life in the lights more

The Music All About You

The last time this happened we were still
friends
It was you, me, and a bottle of wine sitting
on top of your bed
It was going back and forth over every
single detail I could explain
Now it's 6 months later
And I'm sat alone with the same album
getting drunk on a Tuesday

Do you wish you could be here this time
around?
Laugh as I turn the music up too loud
I'd make myself at home like I always used
to do
With the music all about you

Signs of You

A month or so in we sat in the restaurant
Claimed it as ours for that whole autumn
I couldn't even fathom then
That those little wooden tables
Would haunt me 4 months later
No, I don't think I'll ever eat Chinese food
again

A month after that
It was a Friday night
I took the first train home from Dublin
We met up the second I got back
I played you the album
We talked shit and we laughed
Then we took a few too many reckless sips
from your bottle of Jack

You said I'm the perfect storm
And that night I sure was
I got drunk,
And told all the girls in the bathroom that I
was so in love

You got us French fries from the shop across
from the pub where this all began

Sometimes I wonder what life would be like
if you never held my hand

Because now it's a dying language
Used to be a gold rush
All the vultures are getting anxious
Waiting for the final bones to crush

It was early last month
You dealt the final blow
I didn't even cry then
Because there was nothing left to show
Of all that I'd fought so hard to keep
But you were always playing to leave
I kept a running list for months
Couldn't bring myself to put the pen down
You showed off your new life
Like I wasn't your whole town once
But you were a swing state
Only sometimes you called it what it was

And I sure fought my corner
You can very well say that
But I was running dry
I was living in the past

And then one day it all hit me
I got taller, I kept busy

I stopped keeping lists
Can't believe I ever did
I got brighter, I kept moving forward
I stopped searching everywhere for closure
Can't believe you missed your train to
Madrid

I always wonder what life would be like if
any one thing went differently
But I stopped calculating time between you,
me, and your new country

It is the hardest thing
Forgiving someone not worth forgiving
But I honestly think I forgive you now
I couldn't hold it any longer
I introduced myself as an author
And all my dreams are louder now
Took you off the forefront
Made myself more important
And I honestly didn't get it
How love becomes indifference
I see it clearly now

I had to make peace with leaving it all
behind
Charting stars and freezing time

My tears on the letter I gave you the night
we said goodbye
I thought I would always be mourning you
and I
But I've opened up my eyes
I finally see it clearly now

It really was the end of the world
But now I have new things to look forward
to
I quit checking telephone wires for a bird
Stopped looking everywhere for signs of
you

Now I've outdone myself
I really thought I wouldn't make it through
My eyes are mine again
Stopped looking everywhere for signs of
you

Dead Man Walking

He's a dead man walking
Full of angst and misery
He did his best work when he let his body
do the talking
But that was all before he met me

He's a dead man walking
He's committing treason but longs for peace
His heart laid in a chest
And I got the only key

He's a dead man walking
He's a charmer and a cheat
He is never going to forget me
That much I'll guarantee

I'd meet him at world's end
And we could do it all again
…
Now I can't wear some of my clothes
Because they still smell like his cigarette
smoke
And we are no longer talking
Now he's a dead man walking in a shiny
new city
And I'm hollow

Lost at a roaring sea
Casting sails on the ship he jumped from
Maybe one day he'll come back and say he
really was in love
But I'll probably be dead by then

Please!!!!!

You celebrated with me the night I finished
college
You joked that now I'm officially an
alcoholic
And forced to stay nostalgic

You told me I could do it all
Write what I want
And work a 9 to 5
But for you drop my whole life
And come running the second you call
Because you swore you'd never leave me
behind

I wake up
And it's quiet everywhere
Think I hear your echo
So all I do is stare
At the pile of clothes in the corner of my
room
That are shaped just like you

I laugh it off
Submerge my thoughts in my third drink
I think I might call you
Do you want to talk?

It's been 135 days
Since I last saw your face
Actually almost got on a plane
I cleaned a whole house across the street
from a farm
Just to make a little money
God, you still have me in the middle of your
palm
Jumping off the deep end
Because I heard you got new friends
And I feel like I might die

Look at me now
I'm doing the big things we always talked
about
But I'm on some therapist's couch
Still secretly hoping I'll see you in a crowd
I got my degree in the mail yesterday
But I'd send it all back just to see your face
Wish I could say that's a lie but it's not
Look at me now
Running back to the back lot
I'll meet you there
If you want to talk
Please say you want to talk!!!!!!

Snow Globe

I think we were living in a snow globe
Every day was our own little universe
It became our little home
We lit a match inside the both of us
Reflecting off the glass it was luminous

Those raindrops mimicked artificial snow
Swirling in circles and taking different
routes
But always crashing back into each other
I don't think I'll ever recover
And I don't think you'll ever find another

A perfect scene behind thick glass
Crossed our hearts just like our paths
We didn't have to think about what came
after
Until we picked a new place on the map

That trip we took was nearly a disaster
All our pictures we took at the top of the
clock tower
A miscommunication in the hotel, repeated
disavowals

We were chain linked on pedestals

Going back and forth over flower petals
Living under a spell, another black market
scheme
Falling like snow, all our movements
glittering
Black t-shirt and lilac floral sheets
Everywhere we went we saved each other a
seat

We were each other's safe haven
Conversing in our secret language
Months of self-imposed isolation
We were all we ever needed
Playing doctors healing all our broken
bones
Getting high off cigarette smoke and hope
We were living in a snow globe
Handcuffed to being this close to someone
Months of dreamscape illusion
Playing pretend in our seclusion

Handcuffed to all our possibilities
Everything was what we needed it to be
Bottles, pages, and cobwebs brushed off the
caverns of our minds
What a magical, effervescent time

It was once in a blue moon

Down the train tracks we went to the zoo
Watched my phone take pictures of you
It was a perfect simulation
I colored your imagination
Watched your phone play songs from
'reputation'

We were untouchable
Spinning in a scene that role-played home
That rainy season mimicked artificial snow
Living in a snow globe

Kind of Love

I know you found it poetic
Us trapped in a mirror maze
Reflection of truth in your face

You know that you meant it
And I took it as the highest praise
Because I chose you
And you chose the same

Talked each other through
All the things we could ever think up
A sounding board, our own little club

You're a January baby
With a falsely earned god complex
And a reckless obsession with being a
perfectionist
But I'm the only one at this party who
knows you're too soft for all of it
You try to be humble and not act like a
cynic
You're a lunch-under-the-bleachers-type
who is incredibly psychoanalytic
You have a fear of getting too close
You quickly get tired of fake smiles and
people you have to mimic

You ignore every sunrise, sleep with the covers over your eyes
An electric fence tightly wound around your heart
It was your best shot at a defense mechanism
But when you met me that all fell apart

Isn't it strange, all the things I still know?
Whispers of our monologues in the place you called a dungeon
When you held my hand over the phone while I was in London
Isn't it strange when people become home?

It was an emotionally explicit kind of love
To forget the things you said you'd have to cut out your tongue

Is there any one reason why you left me for dead?
We introduced each other as friends
But I died for the whispers in between the lines
The echoes of too many late nights I couldn't retell with the same effect
All my friends tried to get me to run with scissors just so I'd cut the thread

There is no reasoning with me and my list of
reasons
The hill I die on is all you gave me to
believe in

I crash my own party hiding in plain sight
We haven't spoken in days
But I think it's finally time
I ran in circles, down the stairs spilling my
white wine
Been craving more of our reckless nights
You follow me out to our spot under the bike
racks
I feel so out of it while being all in
This is the last moment it goes unsaid
Can't take it back

So I confess all my whims
Echoes of foreign city street band violins
I'm giving you everything I have on a silver
platter
We both are wise enough to know
That the winds will scatter us to the poles
But I am hellbent on your soul
Your name etched on my bones
I cut off my nose; and you did too
It is a cosmic fucked up twist of fate

Now look in the mirror and say it to your
face
Don't be a coward
We talked about it for hours
You know what it was
It was an emotionally explicit kind of love

You call me a masochist
Like I want to keep fighting with my fists
Just re-hold my hand
And it will all be fine

You blame the drinks and the drugs
I blame you and that one pub
To forget the things you said you'd have to
cut out your tongue

You told me it's not personal if we don't talk
much anymore
As if there isn't an indentation from the
same spot where you'd knock on my door
We were always slinking through the night
And hiding away
Those nights we'd go out and we couldn't
separate
And even when we did
We were always keeping lists
And holding out till we could meet up again

Because it was emotionally explicit

Why'd you have to tear it down?
You say I dragged it out but you dragged us
through the mud
You know it was love
You're sinking with weights on your ankles
So why'd you dive in knowing all that you
did?
There on the river bridge
We photographed something we'd never get
back
That whole city feels like somewhere I've
never been
Even though we ran up the castle steps to
the overlook
You told me to put the red roofs in a song
I'll do you one better
Here's a whole book

You curse me out as you curse yourself
Told me I saved you from hell
I know all your secrets
I live inside your mind
I know your next move
I know exactly which line
You're going to cross

You said I'm the only one who saw the real
you
So I died for our language and bled out the
proof
Now you self-isolate like a protected
witness
But I know that you really do miss this
It was all so emotionally explicit
And I hope you cut out your tongue
Because it was
Love,
   The Masochist

Victorian Ghost

You hold me in highest regard
But you were nothing but a pack of cards
I was just a puppet on a string
Our paths intertwined by a benefactor I
addressed as the universe working its magic
But a crinkle in the fabric didn't flush out
Frozen clocks and statues crumbling down

So you snuck into houses through windows
left open
By a girl on the windowsill feverishly
hoping
That one day you'd empty your pockets and
put down your sword
And surrender your truth and maybe even
your heart

I didn't fit into your lost boy legislation
I fell hard for your charms and persuasion
I turned to stone waiting for promises to
keep
Fluttering through memories now scattered
like stars
But the window pane has rusted over
And looking out feels like a cage with
invisible bars

You fled to preserve your own brittle heart
And nothing seemed fair in the war of all
crimes
Our fate like a wishbone
But our hands were tied
You were promised a fortune if you were
good and true
But that was all before you understood what
it meant to have something to lose

And you flushed out your scheme
I prayed one day you'd outgrow your
tendency to flee
But since I stole your heart you had the get
the upper hand back
Giving your best performance in the final
act

Pining after your treasure island
Even brass shines in the sun
But candelabras rust if no one is around to
light them
I stood frozen in time
Preservations of what once was mine
Matches and lighters sinking in rain puddles
Faded like all of my best colors

You grew tired of the moors where I came to
life
You wanted a city to make you feel alive
So you took a step back with your head in
your hands
I hoped you'd write and I wouldn't hermit in
the hills we once ran
So I danced with your echo in grand
hallowed rooms
Bickered with our conversations from
former moons
An existential state of doom

I forgive you for the world you wanted to
explore
For the timing you despised even more
For the riches you had at your fingertips
The adventures on the biggest ships
You were just a twenty something rogue
This is how the story always goes

But love is never a waste
When it changes how your world is shaped

Lost to the pages of my glittering youth
I don't know who'd I'd be if there hadn't
been you
I comb through the stories like a historian

Books with edges wilted from old flames
X-s crossed through all of your names
Monologues and verses so stained with
fallen tears
That the characters in ink have disappeared

But this story is set in stone
In the depths of all your bones
I haunt all your stories
Like a Victorian ghost

London Fog

Just because I've written you out of my
system
Doesn't mean I don't still have symptoms
I still miss it
And all the good that we did for each other
I wish I could know you in summer
But my face is finally getting back its color

We couldn't be kept apart
From a hand hold to a wave goodbye
The London fog was the breath of fresh air I
didn't want to admit that I needed
It's a brutal confession, but I pleaded with
the sky
To keep our stars crossed
But now that life we had together is my
biggest loss

As the frost sets blue on Notting Hill
I tell myself I'll forget you
But I know that I never will

You did everything I never would have
I would have made this last
You did everything you swore you never
would

Now I guess you're gone for good

All signs of you were there in the London
fog
So I can't play dumb like I did in Prague
I did everything you called me out for
You could always see through all of my
darkest blue
There was no one else I adored as much as I
did you
I could always see through all of your
masquerades
We were twin flames
In the wrong shade

The fatality is all that life I got to live
But now there's nothing more for me to
give
Waving goodbye to a place I could have
lived till the clock broke
I've been breathing mountain air, now no
more smoke

Down the rabbit hole spinning
I will always miss it
But I've scattered the ashes in the name of
something tried and true

A moment of fate
That I'm eternally grateful for
But our story has run its course

ACKNOWLEDGMENTS

Writing this book was truly the most cathartic and healing process I have ever gone through. I am extremely thankful to everyone who helped me bring this book to life.

To Erin, for living out every moment of this book with me. For being the best editor and for being a true friend. This book would not be possible without your dedication to the craft or your dedication to being friends with a hopeless romantic.

To Maha, for being a loyal listener of the heartbreak and for designing the cover of this book. Your talent will always amaze me.

To everyone who is a valued member of 'Delulu Nation'; to every debrief, laugh and tear. The love runs immensely deep.

To my family, for believing in me and my storytelling, and most of all for supporting me through every dimension of my heartbreaks.

And to every boy mentioned in this book-thank you for making me a writer.

Made in the USA
Columbia, SC
13 July 2024

38584164R00085